This Book Belongs To:

....

....

Find the Difference

Could you find 10 differences between these pictures?

Connect the Dots

Connect the dots to complete the picture and color it for fun.

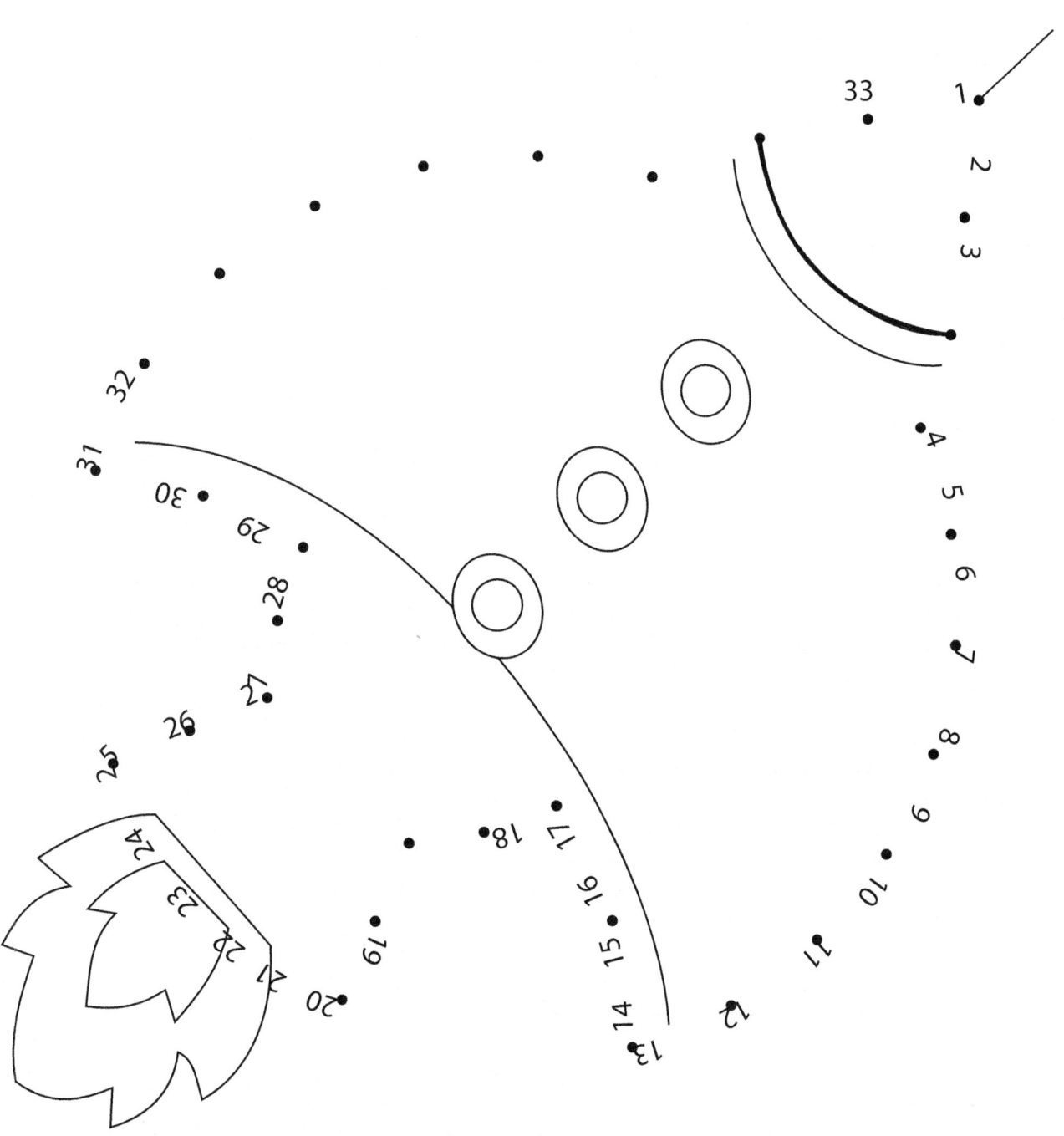

Connect the Dots

Connect the dots to complete the picture and color it for fun.

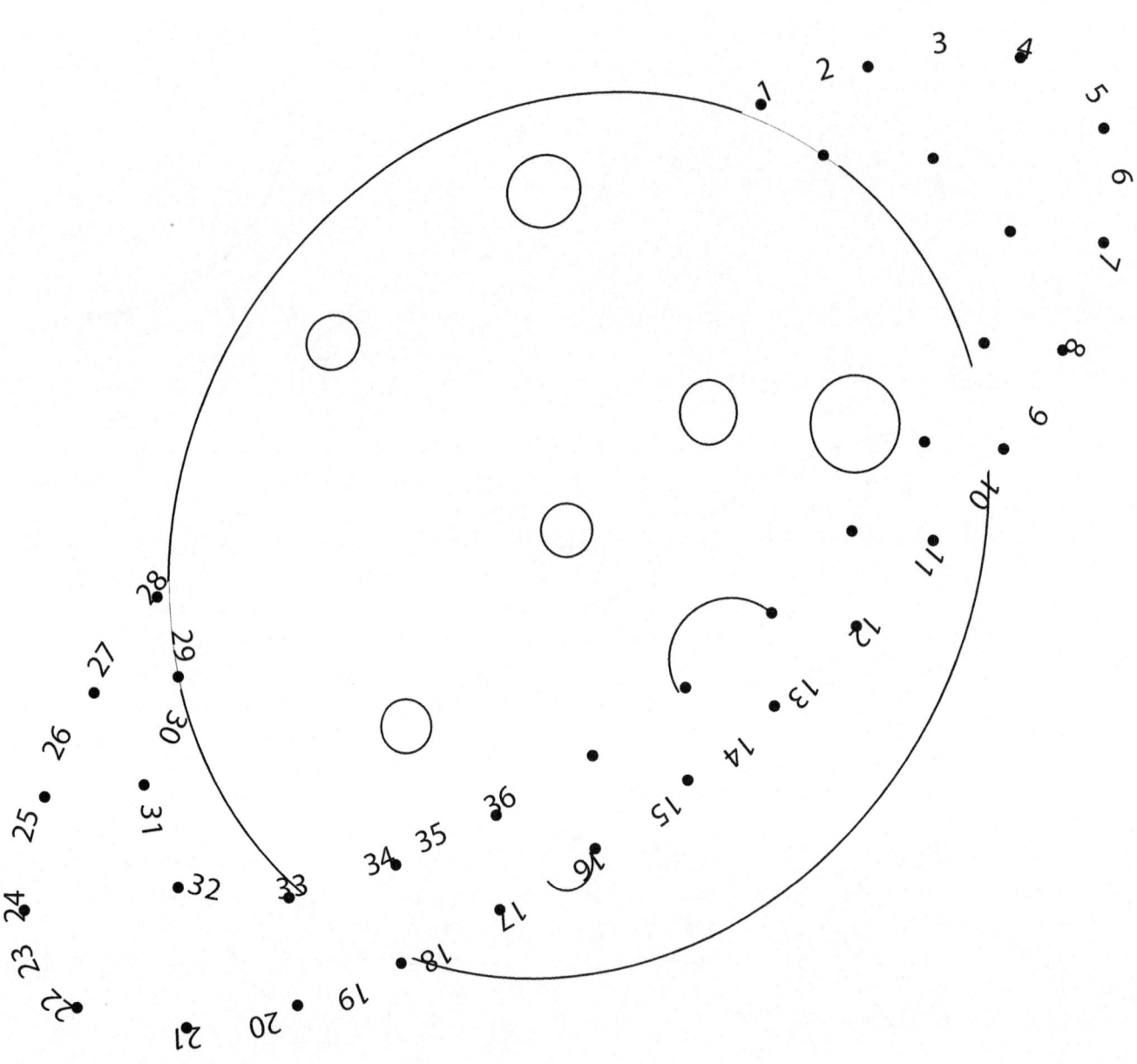

Find and Write

See the picture. Write the name of each object.

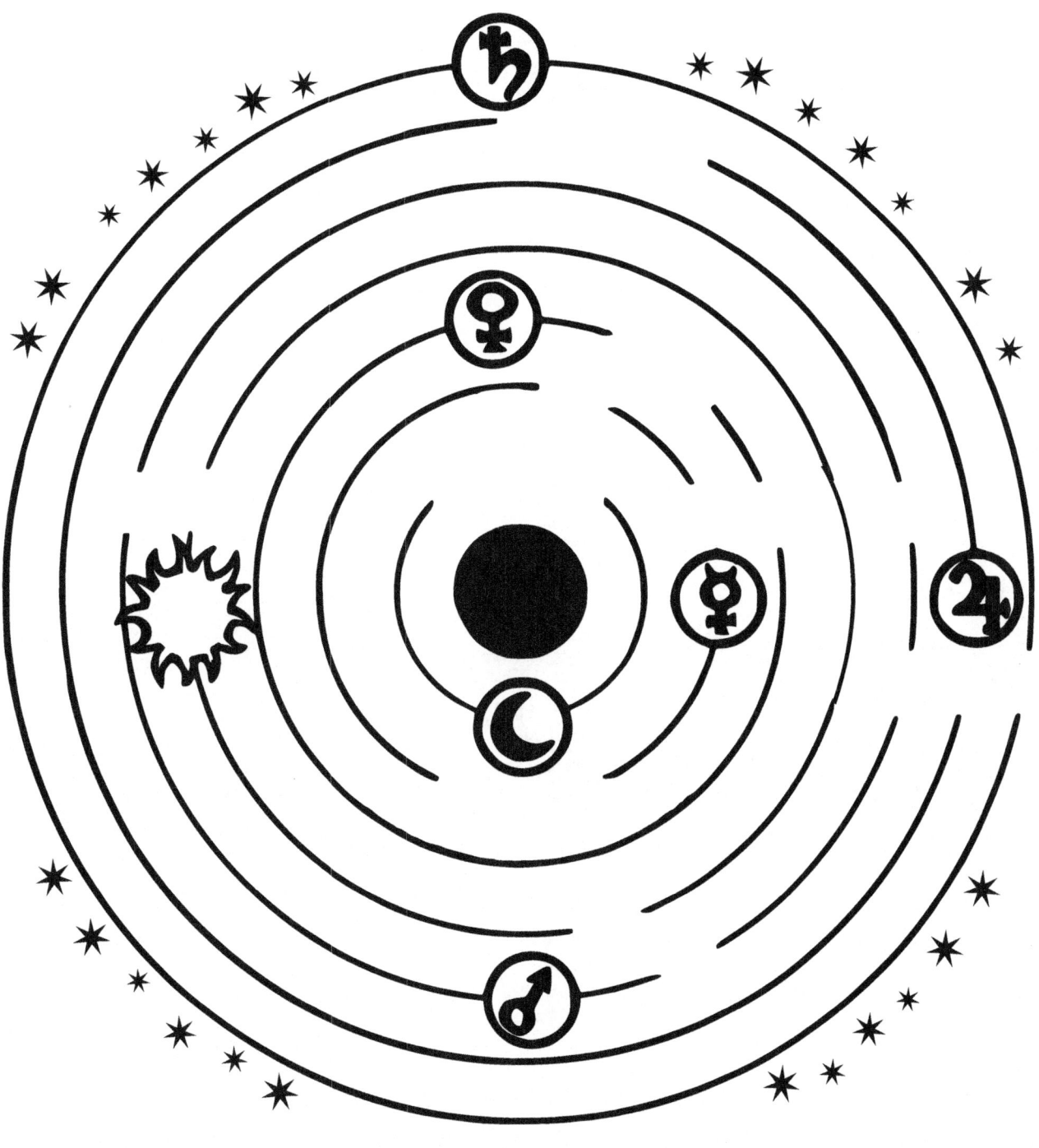

| Sun | Saturn | Moon | Mars | Jupiter | Mercury | Venus | Earth |

Scramble Words

Unscramble the words with the help of the pictures given below.

LENA _____

PEACE _____

MONO _____

STARS _____

UNS _____

HEATER _____

CTKROE _____

AHCPSISPE _____

SWARM _____

TMCOE _____

Maze Challenge

Find a way through the moon maze.

Maze Challenge

Find a way through the spaceship maze.

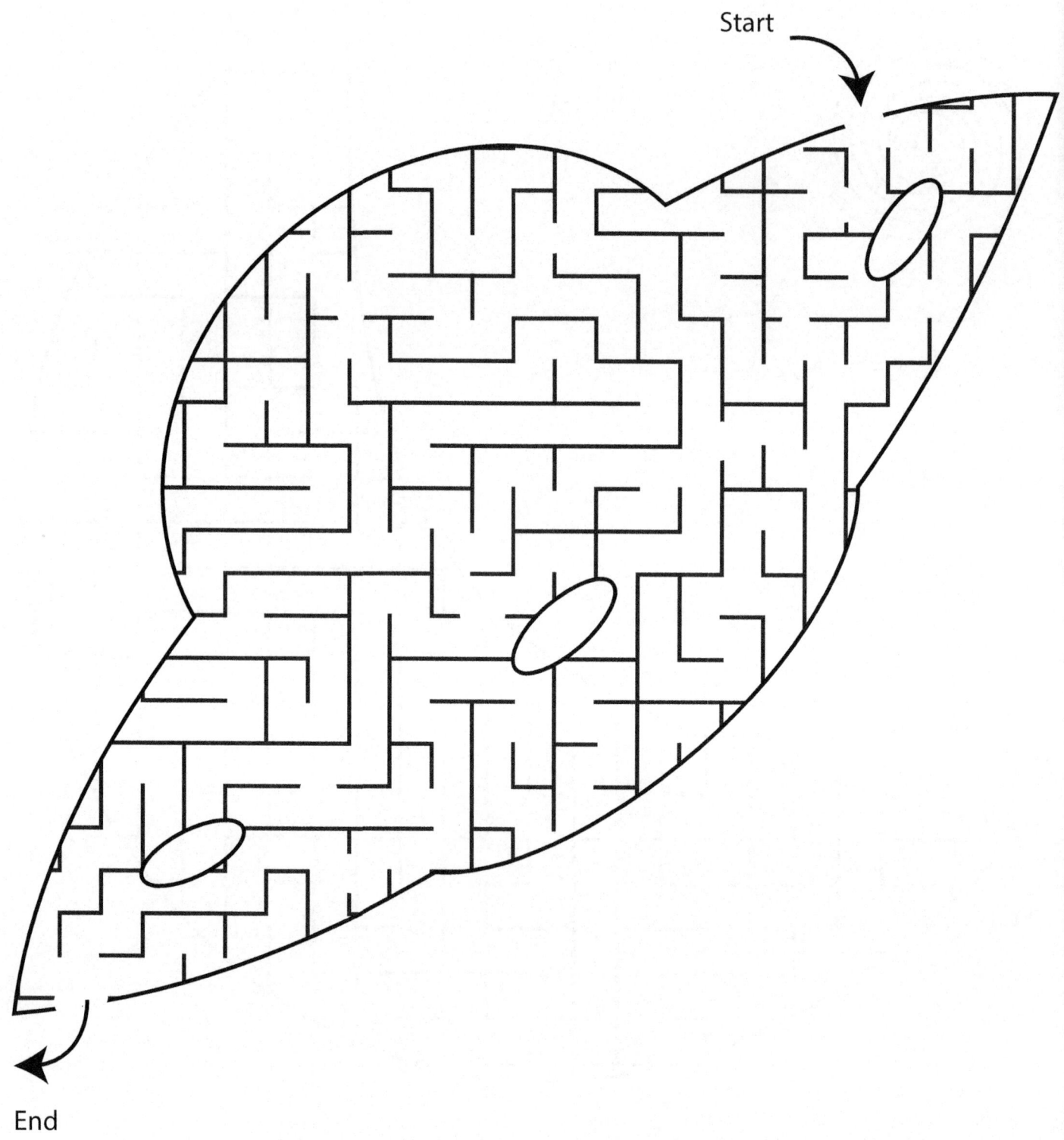

Maze Challenge

Find a way through the robot maze.

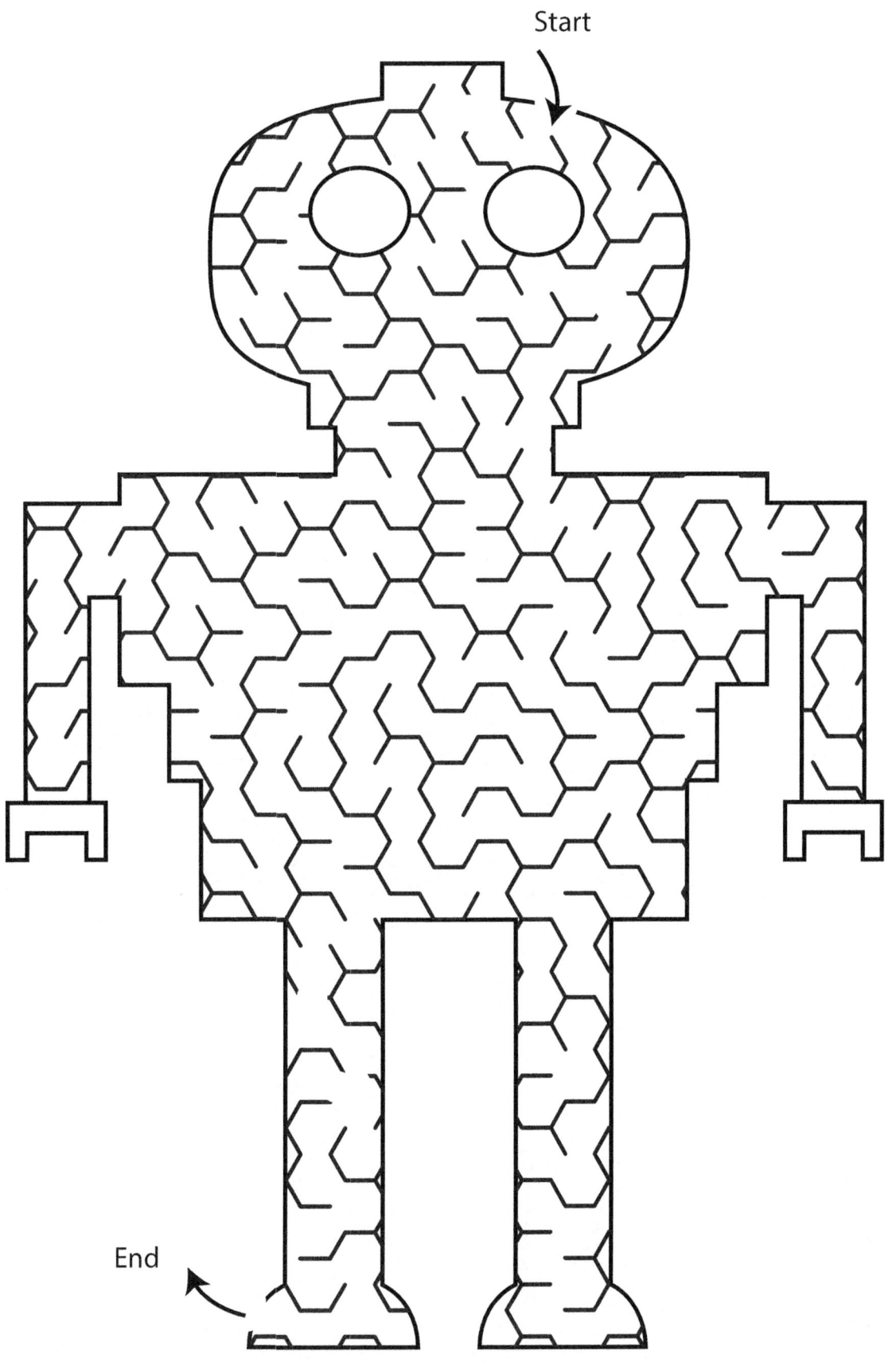

Maze Challenge

Find a way through the rocket maze.

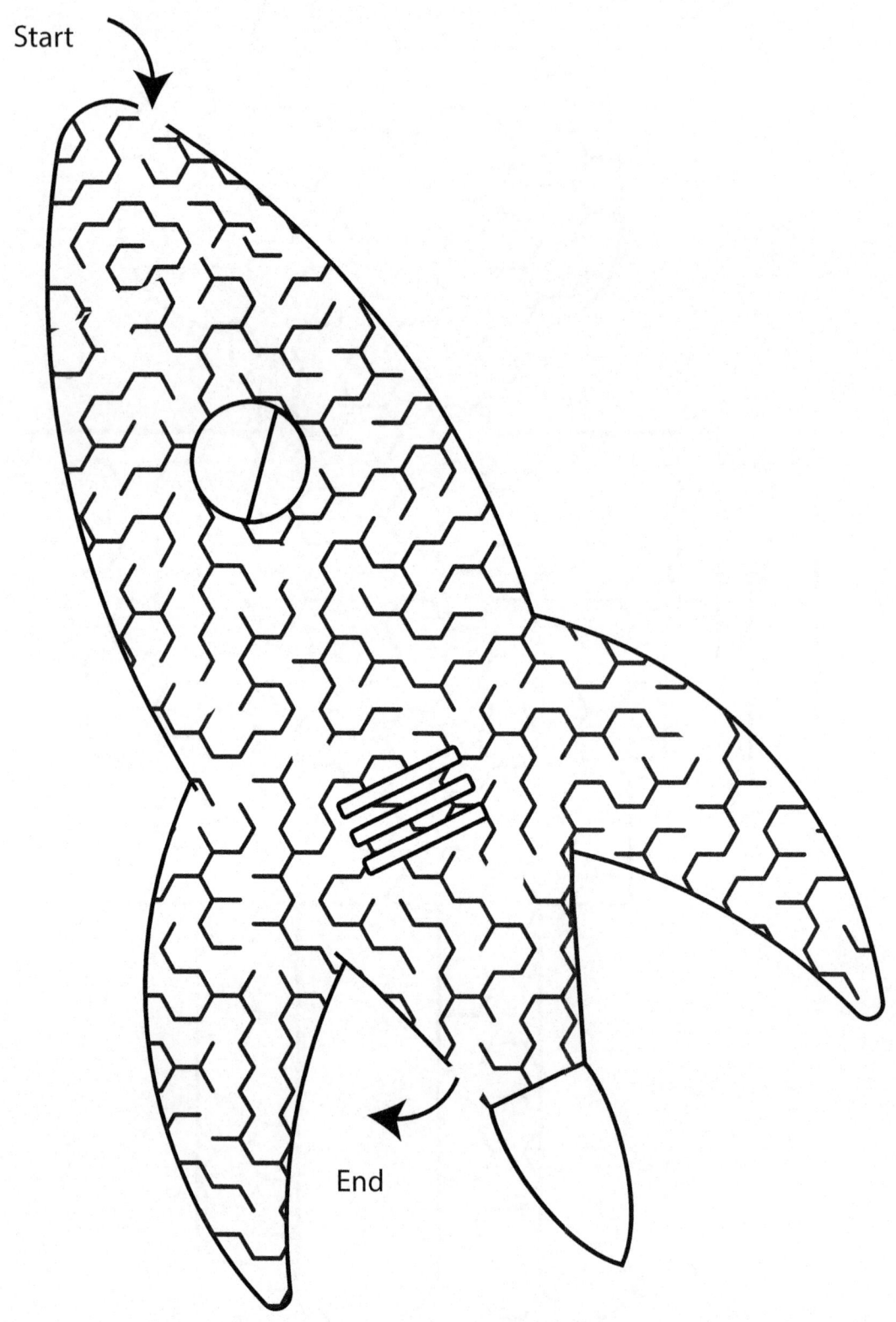

Maze Challenge

Find a way through the star maze.

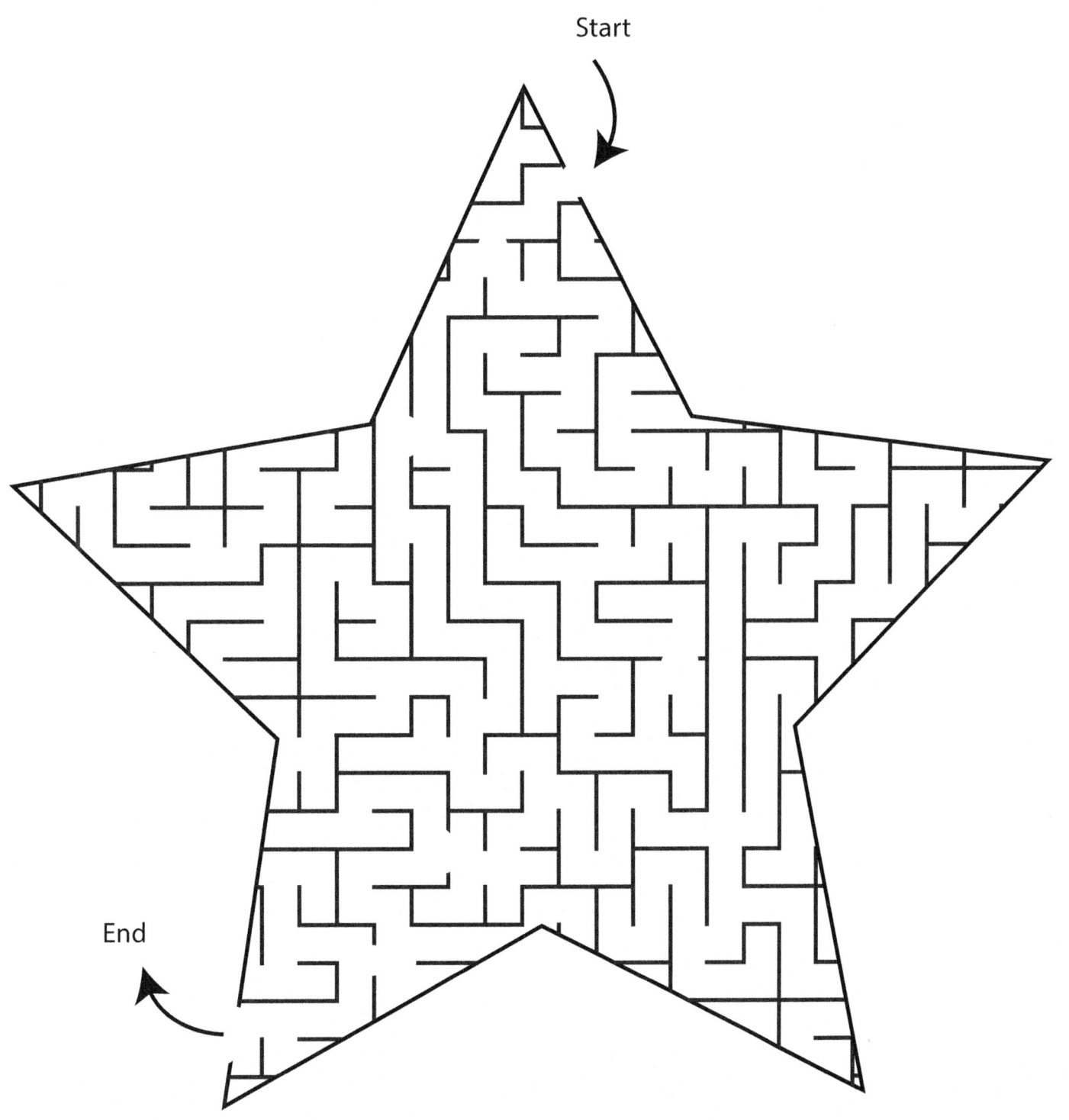

Word Search

Find and circle all the hidden words listed below. Words can be up, down, or forward.

S	T	A	R	G	C	O	M	E	T
F	A	G	H	P	L	A	N	E	T
G	J	R	G	Q	M	X	A	Y	B
R	G	A	L	A	X	Y	L	D	E
C	W	V	J	M	V	M	A	S	E
X	S	I	V	A	P	K	O	P	R
E	X	T	J	R	P	N	V	A	C
T	N	Y	P	S	X	S	B	C	D
P	E	A	R	T	H	U	Y	E	F
R	O	C	K	E	T	N	Z	F	G

SPACE GALAXY
ROCKET EARTH
PLANET MARS
STAR   GRAVITY
COMET SUN

Word Search

Find and circle all the hidden words listed below. Words can be up, down, or forward.

B	L	A	U	N	C	H	V	X	I
D	O	N	T	N	L	M	O	O	N
O	O	W	J	P	L	U	T	O	V
R	B	Y	W	S	K	Y	L	A	B
B	Y	V	E	N	U	S	S	D	A
I	P	L	A	L	I	E	N	O	P
T	M	L	U	N	A	R	F	U	Q
N	H	B	V	B	S	P	V	J	W
A	S	T	R	O	N	A	U	T	N
G	M	M	E	T	E	O	R	J	L

LAUNCH   METEOR
ORBIT   MOON
LUNAR   ALIEN
ASTRONAUT   PLUTO
VENUS   SKYLAB

Word Search

Find and circle all the hidden words listed below. Words can be up, down, or forward.

```
Y  Q  W  S  H  U  T  T  L  E
A  O  U  T  E  R  C  L  F  C
Q  I  B  I  G  B  A  N  G  L
J  R  S  N  M  L  H  P  P  U
S  N  E  B  U  L  A  J  G  S
B  A  S  T  E  R  O  I  D  T
Q  N  E  P  T  U  N  E  Z  E
V  M  I  L  K  Y  W  A  Y  R
Y  G  O  M  E  R  C  U  R  Y
B  L  A  C  K  H  O  L  E  V
```

OUTER
ASTEROID
NEBULA
MERCURY
NEPTUNE

BLACKHOLE
MILKYWAY
SHUTTLE
BIGBANG
CLUSTER

Word Search

Find and circle all the hidden words listed below. Words can be up, down, or forward.

X	S	P	S	O	X	Y	G	E	N
P	N	K	A	N	A	S	A	J	R
U	R	E	T	I	F	K	L	L	Q
T	B	P	E	F	E	Y	I	M	G
M	R	L	L	Q	Z	K	L	Q	A
L	A	E	L	Z	C	H	E	K	S
E	Y	R	I	M	J	U	O	T	M
M	S	A	T	U	R	N	Q	T	R
N	C	I	E	S	O	L	A	R	D
I	E	U	K	M	O	K	Q	S	R

RAYS
OXYGEN
SATURN
SATELLITE
SKY

SOLAR
GALILEO
NASA
GAS
KEPLER

Word Search

Find and circle all the hidden words listed below. Words can be up, down, or forward.

G	S	D	D	W	K	N	V	E	S
U	T	C	E	I	O	F	E	I	U
N	A	O	E	A	I	U	N	L	P
I	T	S	P	J	C	W	U	E	E
V	I	M	S	H	E	O	S	C	R
E	O	O	P	U	G	R	R	L	N
R	N	N	A	X	I	L	I	I	O
S	P	A	C	L	A	D	N	P	V
E	S	U	E	J	N	S	G	S	A
C	F	T	T	T	T	I	S	E	P

RINGS
STATION
SUPERNOVA
UNIVERSE
WORLD

VENUS
COSMONAUT
ICE GIANT
DEEP SPACE
ECLIPSE

Crossowrd

Complete the crossword puzzle by filling in the appropriate letters with the help of the pictures listed below. Color them for fun!

Crossowrd

Complete the crossword puzzle by filling in the appropriate letters with the help of the words listed below.

MARS
ROCKET
PLANET
MOON
METEOR

PLUTO
OUTER
MERCURY
TELESCOPE
SPACESHIP

Crossword

Complete the crossword puzzle by filling in the appropriate letters with the help of the pictures listed below. Color them for fun!

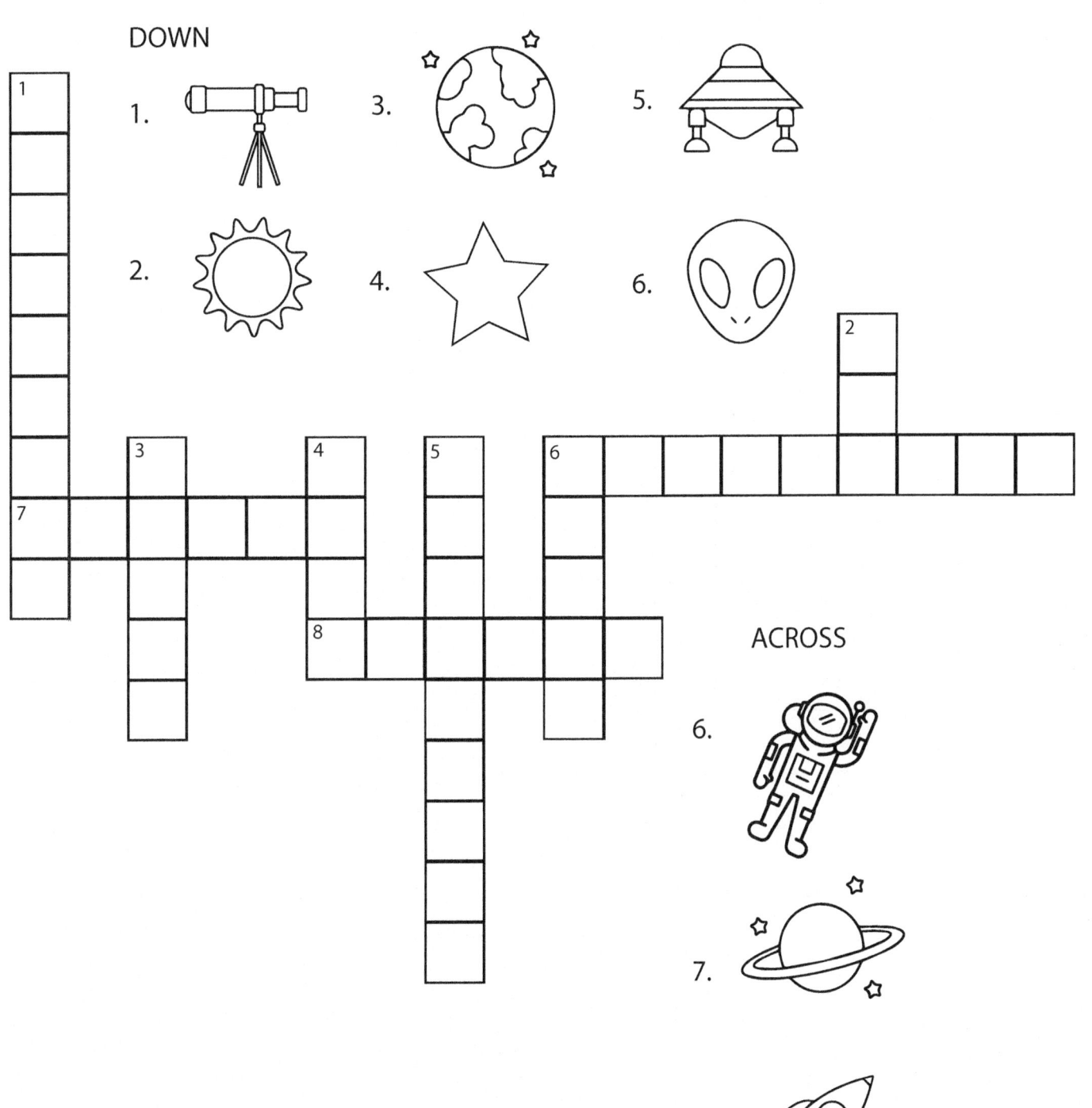

Crossword

Complete the crossword puzzle by filling in the appropriate letters with the help of the words listed below.

NEPTUNE
OXYGEN
COMET
GALAXY
SPACE SUIT

ORBIT
UFO
GRAVITY
SATURN
JUPITER

Crossword

Find and circle all the hidden words listed below. Words can be up, down, or forward.

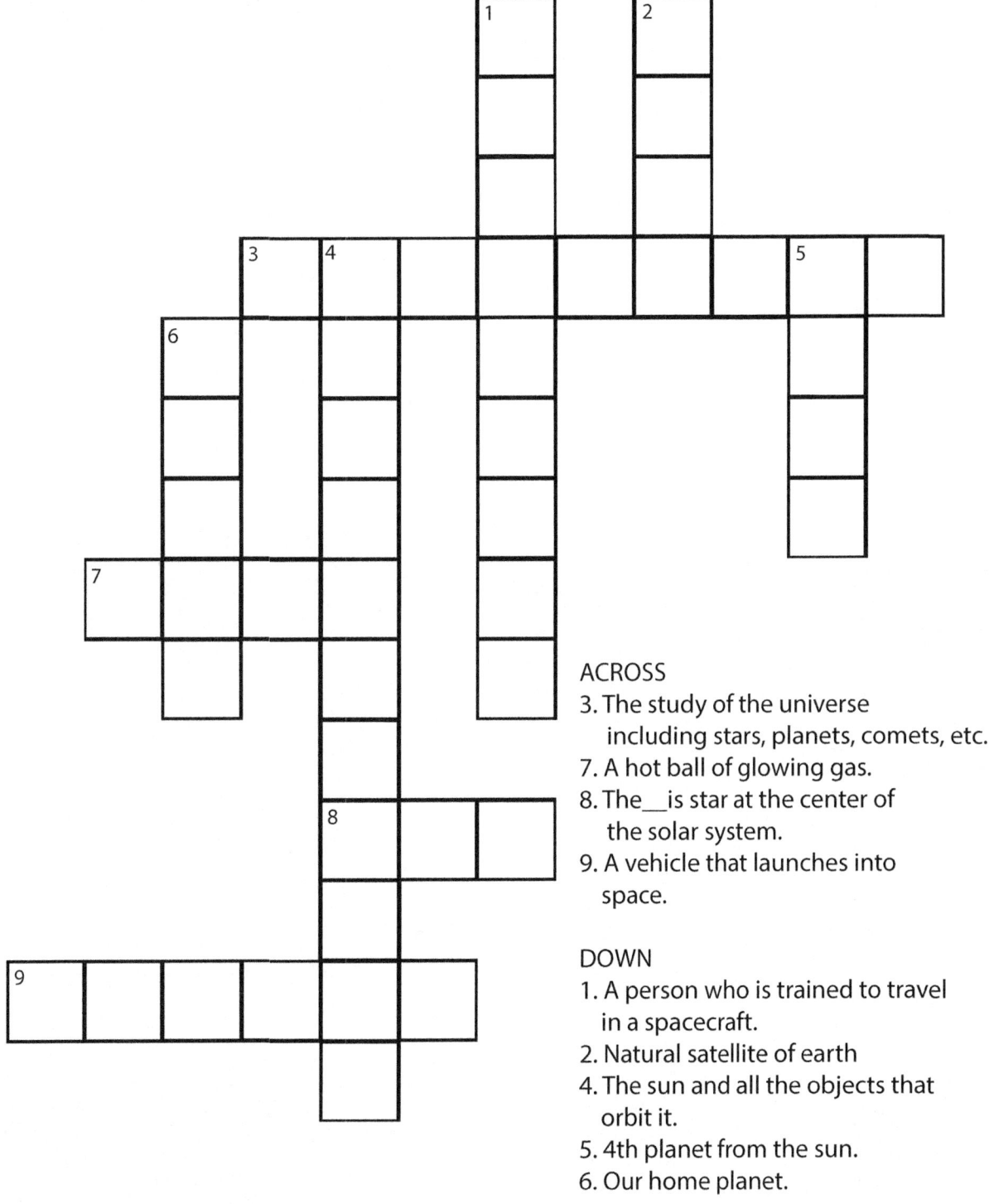

ACROSS
3. The study of the universe including stars, planets, comets, etc.
7. A hot ball of glowing gas.
8. The __ is star at the center of the solar system.
9. A vehicle that launches into space.

DOWN
1. A person who is trained to travel in a spacecraft.
2. Natural satellite of earth
4. The sun and all the objects that orbit it.
5. 4th planet from the sun.
6. Our home planet.

Match the Number

Draw a line from the number to the matching set of objects.

2

4

3

5

8

Counting

Count the objects. Write the correct number in the box. Color the objects for fun.

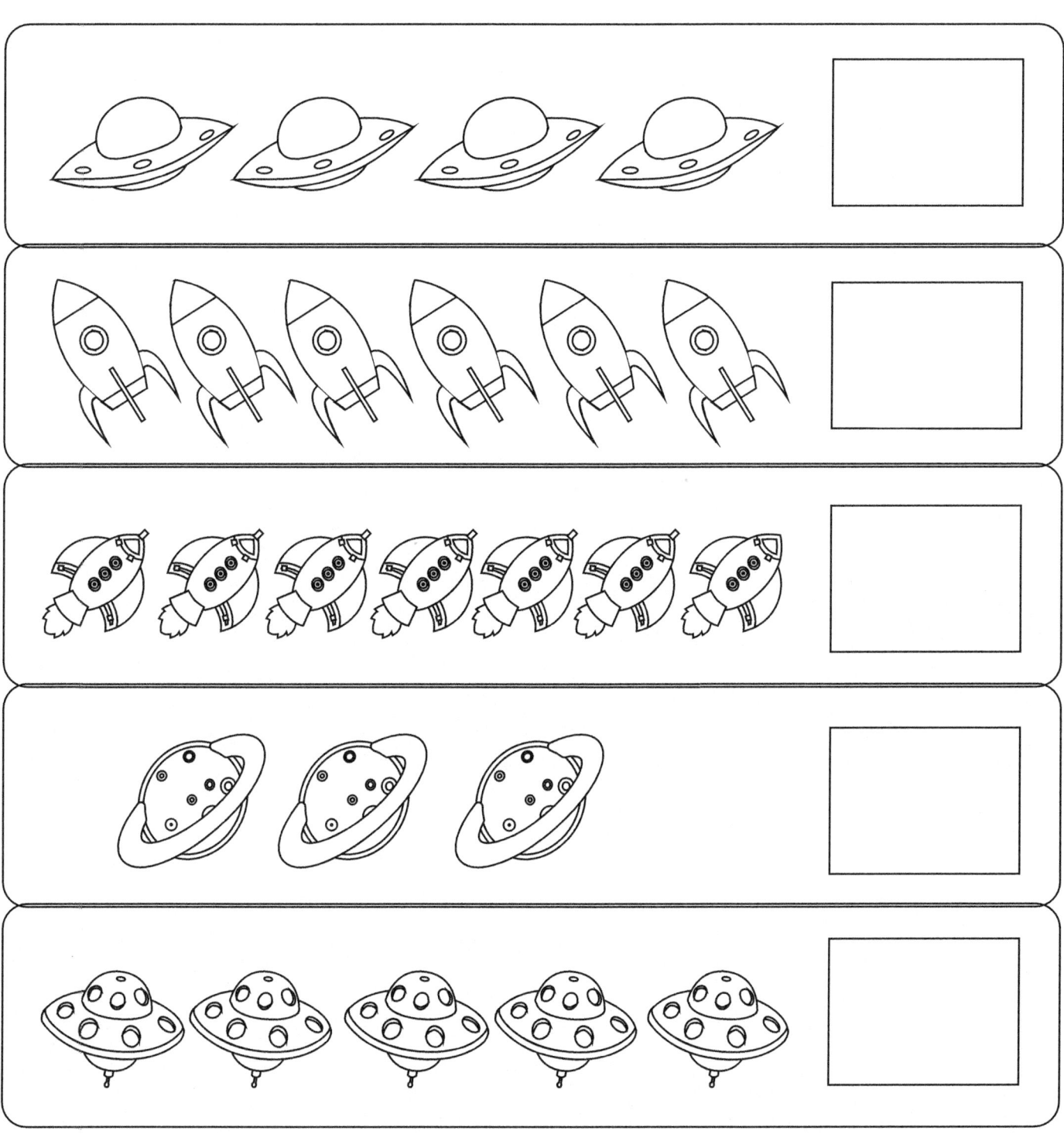

Coloring Addition

Find the answer to each problem and write in the given box. Use the numbers to color the pictures.

6 + 3 = ☐   Yellow   5 + 2 = ☐   Blue

4 + 4 = ☐   Green   8 + 2 = ☐   Orange

2 + 2 = ☐   Red   3 + 2 = ☐   Pink

Subtract Numbers

Find the spaceship. Subtract the numbers in each box and color the spaceship with the correct answer.

6 - 3 =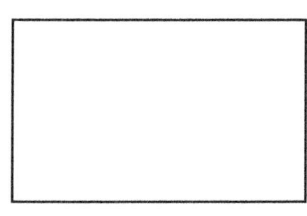

8 - 5 =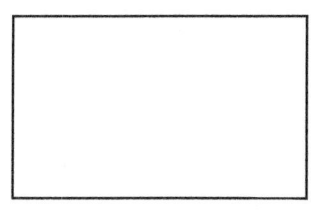

4 - 2 =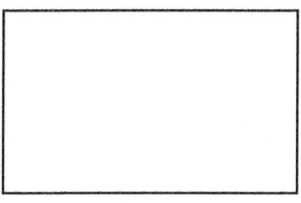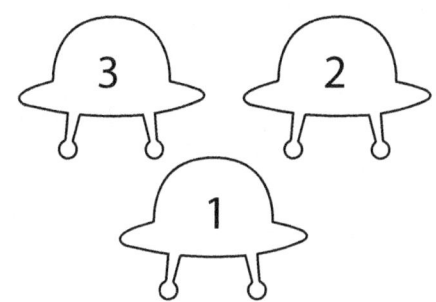

9 - 2 =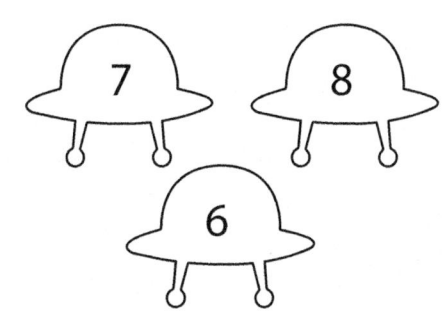

Missing Numbers

Can you fill in the missing numbers by launching rocket to the space?

Connects the number to the image

5

2

8

6

3

Connects the number to the image

1

2

3

4

5

Connects the number to the image

1

5

4

2

7

Connects the number to the image

2

8

5

7

1

Connects the number to the image

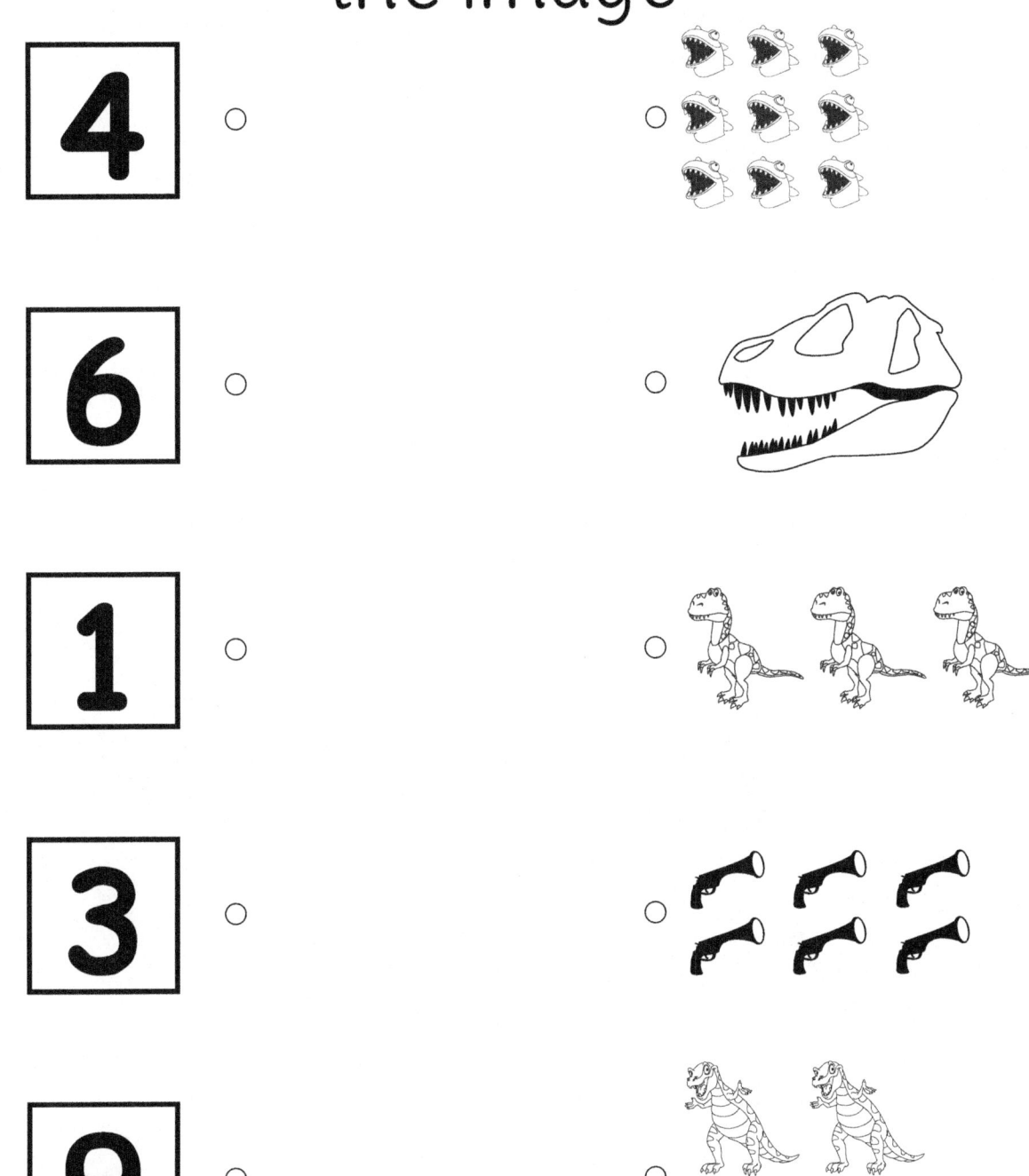

> Please would you like to let your opinion to know your feedback, point of view and suggestion to offer you the best services and products!
>
> You are very estimated for us!

SpaCCEE ActiviTTYY

Printed in Great Britain
by Amazon

36549335R00020